The Bradford Family
ADVENTURES
The Clubhouse Mystery

by

Jerry B. Jenkins

MOODY PRESS
CHICAGO

© 1984 by
JERRY B. JENKINS

Moody Press Edition 1990

ISBN: 0-8024-0807-9

1 2 3 4 5 6 Printing/LC/Year 94 93 92 91 90

Printed in the United States of America

To Cydil, Jenny, and Hannah Van Orman

Contents

1. The Shortcut   7
2. The Shack   13
3. The Metal Box   19
4. A Note in the Night   25
5. Prying Open the Box   31
6. Making a Deal   37
7. Sneaking Back   43
8. Maryann Disappears   49
9. The Surprise   55
10. Visit from Robbers   61
11. "Let's Have the Box!"   66
12. Yo-Yo Faces the Gang   71

1

The Shortcut

Danger was the last thing on Yo-Yo Bradford's mind. She was walking home from school that November day. She had never been bothered by the bullies who stole lunch money and bus fares. But maybe that was because she usually walked home with her brother Daniel.

She wasn't thinking about the bullies. She was thinking about how much her life had changed in a few short months. The year before, when she had been in the third grade, she had been one of only a few Mexicans in her school.

That was hard enough. But she had also been one of the orphans from the children's home. That was worse. They rode the school bus together and had few friends outside their own group. They got called names.

But Yo-Yo liked her nickname. It came from the first part of her first name—Yolanda—and the last part of her old last name—Trevino. It was better than many of the names she had been called.

She didn't know what all the names meant. But she knew they were bad. She had grown to hate the fact that she was Mexican. Even more, she hated the fact that she was an orphan.

She had learned to live with it, though. She became motherly to her little orphan friends. It was because of them that she made herself look on the bright side of life.

Yolanda never wanted her little friends to see her hurt or worried or sad or discouraged. She always told them stories about being adopted. Someday, she told them, some nice new mom and dad would come for them and make them happy. They might even get brothers and sisters—a whole family overnight.

She listened well at school and did all her homework. For some reason, Yolanda was able to understand things better than most people. She had a feeling that good grades and learning a lot of subjects would help make her happier. She knew it would make it easier for her to make friends.

Of course she had been right. Her teachers liked her and said nice things about her in front of the class.

Now as she skipped along, her backpack dangled from her shoulders. She smiled at her unbelievable good fortune. She had been adopted, and by one of her best friend's parents.

She had met Daniel Bradford at the children's home when he came to play with the kids. No one knew what to think of him at first. He seemed like a rich kid. His father was a test pilot who was always going to Florida to work with astronauts. And Daniel lived in a big house in the country with his parents and older brother and sister.

Jim Bradford, a senior in high school, was the best basketball player in town. Maryann was a beautiful, dark-haired sophomore who had already made the cheerleading squad.

Yolanda could hardly believe they were now her big brother and sister. In her wildest dreams, she had never hoped for such a great family. Daniel had become good friends with many of the orphans. Yo-Yo couldn't believe her luck when she was adopted into his family.

Here she was, smaller than normal, a thin, fast-running girl with huge eyes and—everyone said—a beautiful, pearly white smile. And now she was part of a family that loved her.

They were so special. Daniel, of course, was more than her brother. He was her best friend. He was two grades ahead of her, so she didn't play with him and his friends. But after school, on the way home and at home, they were close.

Jim and Maryann treated her nicely. In fact, it was Jim, during one of their monthly family council meetings, who had made her feel so good. She had never even heard of a family having council meetings, but Mr. and Mrs. Bradford never skipped one.

They read the Bible and prayed. And then they talked about lots of things. Any of the kids, from Jim right on down to Yolanda, could say anything they wanted. One night Jim had said, "I think Yolanda ought to have her real last name as her middle name—when she's officially adopted, that is."

"You mean I'm not really adopted?" she had asked.

Everyone laughed. "Oh, yes," Mr Bradford said. "It's just that your name changed, and all the paperwork has to be processed. Then it becomes official. Jim, the way it reads now, Yo-Yo's name would officially become Yolanda Maria Lucia Theresa Bradford."

"Why all those names?" Daniel asked.

"For my mother and her mother and her mother," Yo-Yo said.

"And unless you want all those family names," Jim said, "you should just keep Trevino as your middle name. You would become Yolanda Trevino Bradford."

Maryann giggled. "Yeah," she said. "Then we can keep calling you Yo-Yo."

Yolanda hadn't cared one way or the other whether she kept any of her names. She was not happy being Mexican. And she had never really known her own family. But Jim had

9

been wise. He had said that by keeping her first and last name, and adding her new family name, Bradford, she would keep her identity.

Yolanda wasn't even sure what it meant to keep her identity. She wanted to speak up. She wanted to say that she wanted to leave behind her lost family, her sad experiences at the children's home, her name, the Mexican part of her.

But all she could say was, "No, I don't want to keep my name. Can't I have a name like Barb or Jill or Jackie? I just want to be one of the Bradfords."

That night her dad had come to her room after she was all tucked in. He told her he understood what she was feeling. But he asked her to also think about what Jim had said.

"You may not understand now. But someday you'll be glad that you hung onto the Yolanda Trevino that we all love so much. There will always be plenty of time to change your name if you really want to. For now, we're going to just add Bradford to the end of your long, beautiful, Mexican name."

She had turned over on her side, her back to her new dad. She didn't want to hurt his feelings. But she had hoped to quit being a Mexican when she joined his family. She didn't want him to see her cry.

Mr Bradford put his hand gently on her tiny shoulder. "Yolanda," he said, "it's all of you, everything about you, that makes us love you so much. Changing your name won't make you any less Mexican. But, more important, you should never want to be something other than what God made you.

"No matter what any cruel kids say, kids who don't know any better, there's nothing at all wrong with being from Mexico. In fact, it makes you special. You come from a beautiful land with many wonderful people. And you are what you are. Be proud of it."

Her new father also told her not to be too quick to try to forget that she been an orphan. "That will make you care for other boys and girls who are lonely. Remember all those little girls who looked up to you because told them stories?"

10

She nodded.

"Don't turn your back on them and forget them. They are now far away, and you may never see them again. But there are others everywhere who think that no one understands."

"But I understand," she said turning back to face him.

"That's my girl," he said. "Of course you do. And what about the black children and the Indians and the Mexicans?"

"I understand them," she said. "I know how they feel. I care."

"You see? God has a purpose. Don't pretend He doesn't. You're as much a part of our family as any of us now. But you're something more, too. You're special. You were chosen. God gave you to us."

Yolanda was still puzzled and little troubled by how much the Bradfords seemed to talk about God. But she knew some things. They meant it. They believed it. And they loved her.

Now, only a few months later, she was glad she was a Bradford. And happier even that she was still Yo-Yo. Yolanda Trevino Bradford. Mexican. Orphan. Now part of a family.

She had decided that the greatest thing about this new family was how much they meant to each other. At one of her earliest family council meetings, the three older children said they'd like their parents to consider moving closer to town and to their schools.

Mr. and Mrs. Bradford were shocked. They had planned, saved, and worked hard to buy their beautiful place in the country. They thought now that they had adopted a younger child to be friends with Daniel that the problem of living so far from town was solved.

But the children had planned their argument carefully. "We're getting into all kinds of church and school activities," Maryann said. "And it's just too much, living this far away and having to get rides or take the bus everywhere. It's hard for our friends to get out here and then back home."

Jim nodded. "We know you did it for us. And we appre-

11

ciate it and have liked it a lot. But now we'd rather live closer. Would that be possible?" It had been a difficult meeting, with some hurt feelings, mostly on the parts of Mom and Dad Bradford. But that's what the family council meetings were all about. Getting things out in the open.

Yolanda was amazed at how friendly and honest they were, even when they seemed upset or angry. After a few weeks, Mr. and Mrs. Bradford decided that if it was that important to the children they would move closer to town.

And that's why Yo-Yo was walking home from school instead of taking the bus the way her brother had the year before.

And that's why she should have been thinking about the bullies who liked to steal money from younger kids.

But she wasn't. She was only thinking happy thoughts as she decided to take a shortcut through the woods.

2
The Shack

Yolanda strolled absently into the woods about a half mile from her new home. The Bradford house was new to her. But it was new to the rest of the family too.

In fact, it wasn't new at all. It was an old, old, three-story house with a white picket fence. It had a huge, tree-filled yard with lots of shrubbery.

The inside was enormous, too. There were five bedrooms on the two top floors. Each child could have his own. Dad had turned the other into his den. The biggest bedroom was Jim's. The smallest was Yo-Yo's. But even that was bigger than the biggest bedroom in the home for children.

Mom and Dad's bedroom was downstairs. There was also a family room, a separate living room and dining room, a breakfast nook, and a cool, damp, dark, but fun, basement.

Yolanda kicked at the dead and drying leaves around the trees in the woods.She liked to call it a forest because that sounds more mysterious. It reminded her of the snowy woods that her new mother read to her about in *The Lion, the Witch, and the Wardrobe.*

Yolanda was so deep in thought that she moved deeper

13

and deeper into the tall trees. It wasn't that she could ever get lost. She and Daniel had cut through this way many, many times. Today he had stayed after school for basketball tryouts.

She was headed directly through the woods to the busy street that would lead to her road. Soon she was so deep into the woods that the fading sun was blocked out. The noise of the traffic on the streets was too far away to be heard.

It seemed different to her somehow. She saw the familiar landmarks, and felt only a little lonely. She loved the silence. She stopped to enjoy it. She had lived with a couple of hundred other kids so long. If they weren't chattering, they were crying or whining or laughing or carrying on somehow.

In her new family, she and Daniel seemed to talk with each other or someone every minute they were awake. Now, suddenly, she was really alone. She sort of liked it.

She stood still in the middle of the path. She slowly turned her head as far as she could one way, then as far as she could the other way. All she could hear were birds and squirrels in the underbrush and in the trees.

A breeze chilled her. She turned her collar up to cover the back of her neck. She was adjusting the straps on her backpack when she spotted what looked like a detour off the main path.

The big pathway had been worn down to just dirt, of course. It was hard-packed, dark soil this time of the year. In the summer, it would be dusty. Yolanda promised herself she would return in the summer to see if the deep woods were cooler in spite of the dust.

She had never noticed before any detour off the path. It was strange that Daniel hadn't noticed it either. He had a way of finding such things. They had been late from school enough times because of his exploring or trying to follow an animal or something.

Yolanda wondered if she should wait and tell Daniel about it. She could come back with him to check it out. Or should she take a look for herself? She looked at her watch. There was still time. In fact, by coming through the woods, she had saved a lot of time.

She straightened her backpack once more and looked all around her. There was no one and no sound other than the wind and the animals and the birds.

The new path became harder and harder to follow as she got farther from the main path. Finally she couldn't make out any tracks or matted grass. But it was clear where the detour was leading. Every new step made her crouch lower and lower to avoid overhanging branches.

She edged between fallen trees and stumps. She moved as quickly and quietly as she could in the only direction the cramped area would allow her to walk. She thought about turning and running back along the path again. But she had come this far and she wouldn't be turning back now.

She sensed she was nearing the creek on the far side of the woods. Her mother and father had absolutely forbidden her and Daniel to get near the creek. She thought they were big enough and old enough, but Daniel had never let her talk him into disobeying, at least about the creek.

Soon Yolanda could near the water rushing by. She still couldn't see the creek, but she felt the woods grow cooler and damper as she came near it. Suddenly her new path opened into a clearing. And she didn't know which way to turn.

She started left, but she noticed taller grass that seemed undisturbed. Straight ahead she noted the long drop that would lead to the creek. She headed right, through heavy shrubs, and found herself in front of a tiny shack.

How could she and Daniel have missed this before? She wondered. Then she remembered that she was a long, long, way from their usual path. She crept up around the right side of the building. No one was around—she was sure of that.

She peered in through a dirty window. There were no curtains. But there were dingy lights in the middle of the

15

ceiling in each of the three rooms. She wondered if they worked.

Both front and back doors were locked. And the boards on the rickety front porch were rotted. She thought that someone still used the place. The detour off the main path led here or to the creek. Also, there was a sign on the back door that read: "Keep Out, Bombs, Poison, and Beasts Inside." It didn't scare her.

She decided that the place must have at one time belonged to someone who lived near the creek and fished for his meals. It certainly wasn't big enough for more than two people. That's it, she decided, an old trapper and fisherman and his wife.

Yolanda wondered if there was running water inside. And would it be safe to drink if there was? She could see a sink. But if the last window on the far side was locked—or jammed—as the others were, she wouldn't find out. But it wasn't.

She couldn't believe her luck. From this window, she could see through the front room and out the front window—the one that looked out onto the only entrance to the shack. No one was coming. She was thirsty and wanted to try the faucet. But, most of all, she was dying of curiosity.

With the window raised, she put her hands on the sill to pull herself up. But her backpack hit the window and jarred it loose. It slid down, pinning her half in and half out. Luckily, it had not slid far and had not hit her hard. Still she couldn't move forward.

Yolanda carefully backed out. She reached up to hold the window open as she stepped to the ground. As she lost hold of the window, it slammed down like a guillotine. It really scared her. But she was so thankful that she hadn't had her hand in the way. It would surely have chopped off or broken all her fingers.

If anyone had been close by, he would have come running at the sound of that banging window. She checked her watch again. She should have been home right about now.

She decided that she was only about twenty minutes from home. So maybe she could think of a reason if she was just thirty minutes late.

Her mother wasn't easy to fool, however. She insisted on total honesty. Yolanda might simply tell her the truth. Maybe not the whole truth, especially if she got inside and got a sip of water, but most of the truth.

She scouted around and came up with a thick stick that was large enough to hold the window open. The window was harder to open this time, because it had jammed itself shut. Yolanda yanked on it a while. She loosened it and was able to get it propped open. The time, however, was getting away from her.

She slipped out of her backpack and leaned it up against the shack. As she climbed in, she noticed that the window had a long crack from the top to the bottom. She hadn't seen that before. She wondered if she had done it when she let the window slam. If she had, anyone who lived here would notice.

Yolanda climbed down from the gritty kitchen counter. She noticed the smell of the place. Stale. Musty. She doubted anyone used it anymore. She tried the water faucet. Nothing.

She looked in the cabinet under the sink. The pipes weren't even connected anymore. But why were there still chairs and a table? And even empty bottles? They weren't beer bottles; they were pop bottles.

Kids played here! She wondered who they were and whether they would welcome a couple more kids.

She explored the other two rooms. She saw nothing but more bottles. No chairs, no nothing! Just rotting old flooring and candy wrappers. Yolanda began to feel strange. She just wanted out of this dirty old place.

She might come back with Daniel another day. But, for now, she was on her way out. The front door had a lock that opened from the inside. But what if she couldn't lock it again? She didn't want anyone to notice that she'd been here, especially if the window had already been cracked and didn't give her away. Anyway, her backpack was outside the kitchen window.

So she went back to the kitchen and started to climb onto the counter again. She hoisted herself up. Then she noticed that two of the cabinet doors were wired shut with an old coat hanger. It had been straightened and then wound around the knobs.

No one could ignore a temptation like that. Even though her heart was racing, and her watch was ticking, and she had the feeling that she was being watched, Yolanda slid off the counter and dropped to her knees in front of the cabinet.

Her fingers ached as she worked to unwind the thick wire.

3

The Metal Box

It quickly grew dark as the sun went down. But Yolanda felt a desperate need to see what was inside the cabinet. Maybe it was nothing but cleaning stuff. Maybe someone had just wired it shut to keep kids out. Well, a coat hanger wasn't going to keep this kid out.

She freed the wire, and the loose doors swung open. It was too dark inside to see anything. She didn't want to reach in without knowing what might be in there. She walked over and turned on the light switch. But the tiny bulb didn't offer enough light to shine under the counter.

What if there are bugs or rats? she thought. She looked at her watch. Much too much time had gone by. She just had to get out and get home. She reached into the window ledge and yanked the big stick out, forgetting to hold the window.

It crashed down again, this time shattering the glass. She jumped back to avoid being hit by the flying pieces. Now she was scared. Would the noise bring someone running? She had to get the window open again to get out, because the jagged edges left in the frame would surely cut her or her coat.

She thought about using the stick to break out the rest of the glass. But she was pushing her luck by staying in the shack too long.

Yolanda worked hard to raise what was left of the window. But when she didn't hear anyone coming, she grew brave again. She carefully let the window frame settle back down. Then she used the stick to feel around under the counter.

There was definitely something under there. Something metal. It was big. She couldn't move it with the stick. Was it a bread box filled with something? She tapped on its top.

Smack!

She jumped back and sat on the floor. The stick was still in her hand. Stuck firmly, and dangling from the end of it, was a mousetrap. A new one. One that could have broken her fingers. Was she ever glad she hadn't reached in under the sink.

Yolanda moved onto all fours and squinted under the cabinet again. She shook the mousetrap from her stick and felt around several more times. At last she was sure there were no more traps.

She put the stick aside. Then she reached in with both hands, all the way to the back of the cabinet. She realized that she was in a very dangerous position. Her head was in the cabinet, along with her arms up to the elbows. She couldn't see or hear anything outside it. Someone could come up behind her. She wouldn't know if they did until too late.

But no one had, and she wanted to pull that metal box, or whatever it was, out into the light. Then she could have a look at it. As she wrapped her hands around the back corners of it, she had a sudden thought. *Was that trap there to keep people from taking the box, or are there mice in here?*

That made her shudder. She backed out, dragging the box along the bottom of the cabinet. It dropped heavily the last four inches to the linoleum floor. The corner of the box dug a hole in the floor where it hit. It made a rattling sound

20

as if there were hundreds of coins inside. The box was secured tightly with a padlock.

Yolanda stood and bent over. She tried to raise one corner so she could get her hands under it. She could raise it about a half inch or so. But she couldn't get her fingers under it. Finally she tugged it once more and shoved the stick beneath it. She stuffed her scarf under it, too.

Within a couple of minutes, she had cradled the box in her scarf and was lifting it with both hands. She decided she could get it at least as high as the counter. But she had no idea how she was going to open it. In fact, she knew there would be no time to open it. Since she had to know what was in it, she would take it home with her.

Yolanda reopened the window and propped it up with the stick. She climbed onto the counter and lay down. Then she reached down for her scarf with both hands. She grasped it tightly and she sat up. This dragged the box up the side of the cabinet scratching the old wood surface all the way.

When it was nearly to the top, it caught on the edge of the counter. By now, Yolanda had her back to the wall. She was sweating and aching. She didn't want to drop it, because it would put a huge dent in the floor. But she didn't think she could lift it as high again.

Her arms were shaking as she fought to keep the scarf-wrapped box tucked up under the countertop. With a grunt, she jerked the scarf up as high as she could. The box rattled onto the counter and down into the sink, chipping the sides of the basin.

Without even taking a break to catch her breath, Yolanda wrapped the scarf around it again and slid it up the side of the sink. She pulled it onto the counter and over to the windowsill. She raised one edge of the box up onto the ledge and pushed the whole thing out the window.

The box thudded to the ground. It dug a deep hole in her backpack and pinned it to the dirt. She climbed out, leaving the window up with the stick still holding it. Working furiously, she got her backpack out from under the box. Then she slid the box into the large zippered pocket.

She leaned the pack up against the shack. Then she knelt with her back to it. She slipped her arms through the straps and struggled to her feet, bearing the entire weight on her back.

It made her stagger. Only when she stood perfectly straight, and walked carefully, could she carry it without falling over. She didn't head back toward the detour and out to the main path. She turned toward the creek bank and started toward the main road. Again she had made a wise decision. Just as she moved past the bushes at the side of the shack, she heard laughter and voices and running feet coming up the detour.

She tried to speed up, but that made her almost stumble. She wanted to listen to the voices, but she knew she had to keep going. The box was making its jangling sound. And the weight was making the straps dig painfully into her shoulders.

Yolanda walked as fast as she could. She listened to a group of what she guessed were boys' voices—maybe one or two girls. She heard a key in the door. But she didn't know if it was front or back.

From inside the shack, she heard swearing and angry voices telling one another that the box was gone, that they'd been robbed, that the window was broken. "Spread out! We'll find him! We'll kill him!"

The she heard pounding feet burst from the back door and run in many directions, including hers. She tried to run, but the box bounced. She could feel the straps straining and about to rip. She slowed, praying that she was not leaving tracks.

She began to zigzag through the woods. Finally she heard street traffic. There was no path—and it was dark now. All she could do was follow the sounds and hope she came to a clearing before someone caught up with her.

The sounds of rustling leaves and feet crashing through

the woods made her stop breathing as she hurried between the trees. They would be upon her any second. She didn't know what she'd say or do. If they found the box on her, which they surely would, she would be in real trouble.

But there was nowhere to ditch it.

Two voices, a boy's and a girl's, were close behind her. She leaned forward and lurched into the open, finding herself next to the highway and several feet from a bus stop. She quickly slowed down. It looked like she had just been walking the path beside the woods. Her breath came in huge gasps.

Some adults were at the bus stop. She would be safe if she could only get there. But the footsteps behind her caught up and passed her. Then they turned around to wait for her. She couldn't move very fast, so there was no escaping. And she was too far from the adults to yell. Anyway, they were boarding the bus.

"You just come out of those woods, little Mex?" the boy asked. He was hard looking and about fourteen she guessed. The girl next to him looked as tough as he did, because she was wearing heavy makeup and a sneer.

"I'm going to catch a bus," Yolanda answered. Her voice didn't even sound like her own.

"You didn't come through those woods?" the boy said, trying to peer at her shoes in the darkness. Yo-Yo hoped he couldn't see any dirt.

She shook her head. "Just coming up here to the bus stop."

They looked her up and down some more. "How much money you got for the bus, Mex?" the girl said. She sounded even meaner than the boy.

"Just a dollar."

"You're walking home tonight, sweetie," she said, "Let's have the buck."

Yolanda didn't argue. She pulled a dollar from her purse.

"Next time, have some more money on you," the boy

23

said, kicking her in the shin. She cried out in pain, hoping that would satisfy him. It did, because the two ran off.

It had been all she could do to keep from reaching down and rubbing her leg. But that would have shifted her weight. Then the box would have made her fall, or at least it would have rattled.

She limped toward the bus stop, just to be under a street light. She knew there had to be a lot of money in the box. But without any way to open it, she was, indeed, going to have to walk home.

4

A Note in the Night

Yolanda slumped to the bench at the bus stop. She couldn't lean back because of the huge metal box in the pack on her back. She winced as she pushed against it and leaned forward to rest on the edge of the seat.

At least there was no one there to wonder what she was up to. They had all caught the earlier bus. Her last dollar had gone to the boy and girl. But Yo-Yo was so thankful they hadn't caught her in the woods. They would have searched her for their box for sure.

She breathed deep and hard. She knew she must get started home, which was just four blocks away. She wanted to take her backpack off and rest her shoulders. But she was afraid she wouldn't be able to pick it up again.

It was almost five o'clock. She knew her mother would be worried. Not worried enough yet to send someone out looking for her, but probably worried enough that Yolanda could expect a good lecture when she got home.

A bus pulled up and the driver opened the door, looking at her questioningly. She waved him on, then stood slowly and trudged across the street. The backpack was so heavy, and she was so tired. She wondered how she had managed to carry it this far.

She found herself bending way over to try to support more of the weight on her back. But that just made her legs tired. She walked straight up, then bent over, then faster, then slower.

By the time she took the left turn that would lead to her home, she was moving very slowly. Tears filled her eyes. She knew she couldn't be crying when she got in the door, or her mother would never quit asking questions.

As she walked up the drive, she noticed Jim's car. She also saw a light on in the basement. He was either working on something or had friends over. Maryann was apparently not home yet. And Yolanda knew Daniel wasn't either.

Mom's station wagon was in the garage. But Dad's car was still gone. He usually got home about six. Yolanda waited outside the front door. She wondered if she had a better chance going in through the garage.

She hoped she could avoid her mother until she had changed clothes and gotten rid of her backpack. She decided the front door was best. Mom would be busy in the kitchen.

But her mother had been watching for her, and Yolanda wasn't quiet enough coming in. Yo-Yo heard her calling out of the kitchen, "Yolanda! Where've you been? I was so worried about you."

Yolanda moved quickly toward the stairs. She struggled up the first three. She turned around just in time to face her mother, who was looking expectantly up at her. "I cut through the woods and got a little lost," Yolanda said.

"Well, come here and let me give you a hug! You scared me being so late. And I want you to stop cutting through the woods when you are alone."

But Yolanda stayed on the steps. Her mother stepped up, and Yoland backed away.

"What is it, Yo-Yo? Can't I hug you?"

"It's just that I want to change my clothes first," Yolanda said. "I'm so tired!" And she burst into tears. Her mother came closer, and Yolanda moved yet farther up the steps.

"Well, all right then, dear," she said. "If you're sure you're all right."

"I'm all right," Yolanda said through her tears. She felt so bad that she had to back away from her new mother—the one she loved so much, and who gave hugs that made you feel so special. "Some junior high kids took my last dollar and kicked me. And I had to walk all the way home. I was really so scared. I wish Daniel had been there."

"Oh, sweetheart," Mrs. Bradford said, moving toward her again. But Yolanda backed up the stairs, her back straight, trying to keep the heavy box from showing or jangling. "Did they hurt you, dear?" her mother called after her.

"Not really. I'll be right down, Mom."

Once in her own room, she let the backpack slide from her shoulders to the bed, where it bounced twice and almost fell off. What a noise it would have made on the floor! Her mother would have thought she had collapsed and died.

Yo-Yo was weak and tired. But she quickly changed her clothes. Then she wrestled the box out of the backpack and covered it with extra blankets. She couldn't wait until Daniel got home.

A black mark was forming on her shin. She rubbed it vigorously even though that seemed to make it hurt more. As she stood inside her door, waiting to go downstairs, she felt bad that she hadn't told her mother the whole truth.

Here she finally had everything she had ever wanted, and she was messing it up by keeping something from her mother. But she just couldn't tell her yet. She had to see what Daniel thought—and see if they could find out what was inside the box.

By the time she reached the bottom of the stairs, her older brother, Jim, was waiting. He had a concerned look on his face. "What's this all about, Yo-Yo?" he said. "I want to know who stole your money. Can you describe them? I'll go get them right now!"

He was so big for seventeen, and she was so tiny for

27

nine, that he just picked her up. He carried her over to the couch where he sat her down. He sat next to her.

She shook her head. "I don't know. It was dark. It was a boy and a girl. Both in junior high, I think."

"Same ones who've been stealing from the other kids?"

"I don't know. I never saw anyone get robbed before. And I never saw those two before either."

"Would you recognize them if you saw them again?"

"Maybe. But I just want to forget it, OK? I'll just not cut through the woods again. If Daniel doesn't walk home with me, I'll take the bus."

"That's a good idea," he said, smiling. Then he turned serious again. "But I'd still like to get my hands on them."

That made Yolanda feel good. But she wasn't sure she'd like him to get hold of those kids. He was too big and strong. But maybe they deserved it.

When Daniel arrived home, of course he had to hear the whole story. Yolanda just wanted to get him alone and tell him all about it. But she couldn't. Mr. Bradford got off work in time to pick up Maryann from school. They really made a big deal out of it at dinner.

"I'm just so glad you're all right," Maryann said. Yolanda felt worse than ever about her secrets when everyone was trying to make her feel good.

Dad agreed and even thanked God in his prayer that Yolanda "wasn't seriously hurt and that You watched over her and protected her." He did tell Yo-Yo later that he hoped she'd learned her lesson. She nodded as if she had. But she wondered if she could really keep from going into the woods again. She wanted to know who had a key to the shack, and what they had in the box she had stolen.

After dinner, Maryann made her tell her the whole story again. It was so good to have a big sister who was nice and pretty and really cared about her. But again, Yo-Yo felt she should really tell her everything. But she just couldn't.

Finally it was Yolanda's bedtime. She ran up the stairs and carefully lowered the blanket-wrapped box to a pillow on the floor. Then she sat down on the floor and pushed it under the bed with her feet.

After chatting with her mother and saying her prayers, Yolanda tiptoed out of her room. She slipped into Daniel's and left him a note. "I have something I must tell you. Knock on my door when everyone's asleep. Bring your flashlight. Yo-Yo."

It was after midnight before she heard the faint knock. She signaled that he should come in and shut the door. Yolanda breathlessly told him the whole story.

Daniel didn't say a word. But his eyes were huge in the darkness. He helped her drag out the box.

"How do we get it open?" she asked.

He shrugged, smiling at her as if he couldn't believe she had lugged it all the way home. She could tell he was impressed, and she beamed. "I guess with a hammer and a crowbar," he said finally.

"Does Dad have those?"

"Of course," he whispered, trying to hide his excitement. "But we can't do it here, Everyone will hear the racket."

"So where do we do it? In the basement?"

"No! They'll hear us there, too. I think in the garage."

"How do we get it down there?" she asked.

"You carried it up here, didn't you?"

She nodded.

"Then together we ought to be able to carry it down."

She showed him the tattered backpack.

"That'll be perfect," he said. "We can each hold one strap. But we'll have to be quiet and careful."

"Should we wait until everyone's been sleeping quite a while longer?"

"Nah," he said, "They've been sleeping quite a while. I fell asleep and almost forgot your note. Let me go to the basment first and get the tools. I'll put them in the garage. That way I can see if there's a clear path from here to the garage, too."

"You remember the last time we snuck out to the garage

911749

in the middle of the night?" she asked.

He nodded. "But this isn't like that. After we find out what this is all about, you're going to tell Mom and Dad all about it. Right? Yo-Yo? Aren't you?"

Finally she nodded, but she was scared.

5

Prying Open the Box

B y the time Daniel returned from his scouting trip to the basement and the garage, Yolanda had slid the metal box into the pocket of her backpack again.

"I got a hammer, a screwdriver, and a crowbar," he said. "And I opened the kitchen door to the garage. We can go straight down the stairs, through the kitchen, and out."

"Grab your strap," she suggested.

"Wow!" Daniel yelped as he lifted his end. "This thing must weigh forty pounds!"

"Shh!" Yolanda said. "Now don't hold that end so high. I'm not as strong as you are."

Daniel backed out the door and into the carpeted hallway. Yolanda stepped awkwardly behind him. The heavy bag was between them. As they reached the top of the stairs, they carefully edged into position so they could move down together one step at a time.

Both were sweating as they leaned forward and stepped down. They stopped and steadied themselves after each step. But soon they grew more confident. They reached the middle of the stairs. By now they weren't stopping between steps.

But the bag had begun to swing back and forth between them. Sometimes it narrowly missed banging into the steps.

Yolanda started to giggle a couple of steps from the bottom. And that made Daniel laugh. "Wait a minute!" he whispered as loudly as he dared. "We have to stop."

They stopped on the last step and got control of their laughter. And they let the bag stop swinging. Then they stepped onto the floor in the living room. They moved out into the kitchen and came to the door that led to the garage.

"Show me how you got this on your back, Yo-Yo," Daniel said. "I'll take it into the garage." Without a word, Yolanda helped him set the backpack on the floor. Then she held up the straps.

She pointed to where he should stand. She turned him around and pulled down on his shoulders. Now he was squatting in front of the bag. She guided his arms through the straps. He stood and staggered. He leaned against the door and caught himself just in time to keep from making noise.

"My flashlight is on the ledge inside the garage, Yo-Yo," Daniel said. "You'll need it, because we can't turn on the lights."

He let her step through the doorway first.

"I can't reach it," she said.

"Here," he said, "watch out." He moved to his left and reached high and grabbed the flashlight. But the weight on his back made him lose his balance. He stepped hard off the one cement step between the kitchen and the garage and spun into his father's car. He slapped it hard and loud with his hands to keep from falling.

"I'm glad the backpack didn't bump the car," Yolanda said.

Finally, Daniel was able to edge between the front of the car and the back of the garage. Slowly he settled down between the cars.

"Nobody should be able to hear anything from in here." Yolanda announced. Daniel nodded. He worked the box out of the backpack and studied it from every angle. Yo-Yo held the flashlight. He pulled on the padlock, just to see how strong it was. It was strong. It didn't even rattle.

He wedged the screwdriver between the fingers of the steel curve that led into the body of the lock. He twisted it. The lock didn't even give at all.

Daniel lifted the lock so the keyhole on the bottom faced up. He braced the lock against the floor and the box. He slid the box up against the front tire of his mother's car. He inserted the blade of the screwdriver as far into the keyhole as it would go—which wasn't very far—and drove the hammer onto the top of the handle of the screwdriver.

All that did was wedge the screwdriver deeper into the hole—so snugly that he couldn't pull it back out. Rather than trying harder to pull it out, he decided to drive it farther in.

He tapped gently on the screwdriver five or six times to get it good and steady. Then he began to bang on it. After several slams, he noticed that the key mechanism had been driven about a quarter of an inch into the body of the lock. And, of course, the screwdriver seemed stuck in there for good, unless he could think of something else.

He banged on it ten more times. The hard plastic handle split. Now he had a useless screwdriver deep into a lock that wouldn't budge. He studied the hinges and the lock supports on the box to see if they might be weaker or thinner than the lock itself.

The hinges appeared thick and solid. Daniel didn't think he could get at them with a tool. All he had left was the hammer and the crowbar. And they wouldn't be of much use.

The supports for the lock, however, the round loops of steel that were held tight by the padlock, looked thinner. He whacked at them a couple of times with the hammer. They bent a little. He stood and held the crowbar so its flattened end lay over the support, and the curved end was at the top.

He had Yolanda hold the crowbar in place with both hands. Then he gave it a mighty blast with the hammer. The bar slipped off the support, glanced off the concrete floor, and dug into the side of Yolanda's slippered foot.

She yelped. Daniel dropped to his knees as the crowbar clattered under his father's car. "Oh, Yo-Yo, I'm sorry!" he said. He reached up and put a hand over her mouth so her whimpering wouldn't bring the family. "Did it cut you?"

She shook her head, pressing her lips together to keep from crying. She yanked her slipper off. In the brightness from the flashlight, they saw only a red welt.

"We were lucky," Daniel said.

"I don't feel so lucky, Daniel. I feel like we're not ever going to find out what's in the box."

"Oh, yes, we are," he said, more determined than ever. "Are you ready to help again?"

"Sure, if you're not going to make me hold the crowbar."

He shook his head. He dragged the box to the driver's door of his mother's car. He opened the door but quickly shut it again when the inside light came on. "Bring me that tape over there—the black stuff."

Yolanda found a roll of a electrical tape hanging on a nail on the wall. She tossed it to Daniel. He wasn't expecting that and missed it. It rolled crazily around him and under his father's car.

"I'm sorry," Yolanda said. "I'll get it." As she crawled under the car, she wound up on top of the crowbar. That made her cry out again.

"Shh!" Daniel warned. "Just slide it out here!" She rolled the tape out. It went past him and under his mother's car. Just as he was about to scold her for that, she kicked the crowbar. It slid into him, and he squealed.

"For Pete's sake, Yo-Yo," he yelled, unable to control himself. "Just sit here and do nothing, and we'll both be better off."

He went around his mother's car and brought the tape back. Then he opened the door again. He taped down the button that kept the light off even when the door was open. He turned to ask Yolanda to help him set the box halfway into the car, so he could close the door on it and hold it in place. He saw that she was crying softly.

"I'm sorry, Yo-Yo," he said. "I didn't mean anything. You're a good helper, really. And you're the one who found this box and everything. C'mon, I need your help."

She helped him lift the box onto the floor of the car. It stuck halfway out the door. Then he carefully pushed the door up against it to hold it in place. Yolanda's job was to lean against the door while he ran the crowbar in through the lock and twisted it.

Yolanda backed up against the door and pushed with all her might. Daniel got the crowbar to twist all the way around once. Now the lock was tight against the box and the bar was straight and flat.

He pulled and pulled. But he didn't have enough power to break the metal supports. Then he got an idea. "I'm going to sit on one end of the crowbar," he said, "and pull up on the other end."

"You'll fall."

"I won't fall."

"You'll fall."

He fell. His weight and the weight of the box were too much for Yolanda. The door gave way just enough to lose its grip on the box. It tumbled out, crashing to the floor along with the crowbar and, of course, Daniel.

His seat landed on a corner of the box. As he hopped around the garage rubbing it, neither he nor Yolanda could keep from laughing. All the while they tried to shush each other, but that only made them laugh all the harder.

"I've got one more idea," Daniel said when they finally got control of themselves. "Can you sneak in and get Mom's keys from the kitchen wall without making any noise?"

"I'll bet I won't make as much noise as you just did," she said.

Daniel used his mother's key to open the trunk of the car. He handed the keys back to Yolanda and told her to hang onto them. She put them in the pocket of her robe.

With the trunk lid open, Daniel and Yolanda lifted the box so it rested right where the lid would come down and hold it in place.

He lowered the trunk lid to where it bit into the middle of the top of the box. The harder he pushed to lid, the straighter the box became. "Get on top of the trunk lid." he whispered.

Yolanda climbed up.

"Where are those car keys? he demanded.

She dug into her pocket and produced them.

"Good. Now just hold still while I get this crowbar set again."

When it was in place, he twisted it one half turn until it was again flat. He knew he couldn't sit on one end and pull the other. He'd had enough of that.

He put one hand on each end of the crowbar. He pushed down with his right and up with his left. Was it giving way? It felt like it! He closed his eyes and strained with all his might. His face turned red. The veins stuck out in his neck.

His left hand was moving up and his right hand was moving down. He was certain the metal supports were giving way under all his strength and pressure. He just knew they would soon break free.

This time it just had to work. He had no more ideas.

6

Making a Deal

Slowly, slowly, Daniel pushed and pulled. Everything was moving to the right. When he heard Yolanda quietly sing, "Whooooa!" he looked up to see what was really happening.

From where she was she couldn't see it, but all his work had simply caused the box to turn on its side. This opened the trunk lid even though Yolanda sat on it.

She slowly slid backward toward the car window, calling out as she tumbled. But Daniel couldn't let go fast enough. He released his grip. The crowbar slipped through the lock and clanged to the floor. The box dropped back into the trunk.

Meanwhile, as if in slow motion, Yolanda, let go of the keys. They hit the trunk lid and slid into the trunk through the space between the lid and the back window. As she jerked back into a sitting position to keep from falling on the floor, the trunk slammed shut under her weight.

"Oh, no," she said quietly.

Daniel slid to a sitting position on the floor and buried his head in his hands. "I don't believe it," he said.

"Did I do that?" Yolanda asked. "Was it my fault?"

"Nah," he said. "It wasn't anybody's fault except mine. I should've been watching. I thought I was breaking the lock supports. But I was just twisting the whole box."

"Daniel, look!"

On the floor lay the screwdriver. Daniel shrugged. They'd finally got it out of the lock, but it hadn't done them any good.

"What do we do now?" Yolanda asked.

"Put the tools away and hope we wake up before Mom and Dad."

"Why?"

"Because we have to tell 'em."

"We do?"

"Yo-Yo, we've locked Mom's keys in her trunk. And the box is in there, too!"

"Yeah, but I'm not ready to get into trouble yet."

"Got any better ideas?" Daniel asked as he removed the black tape from inside his mother's car door.

She sat thinking in the darkness. "This floor's cold," she said.

He smiled at her and shook his head. After he took the broken screwdriver—which he would have to explain later—and the other tools back to the basement and returned, she was still sitting there. "Well?" he said.

"I want to see if Maryann will help."

"Maryann?"

She nodded.

"What can she do?" he said. "She doesn't have keys to Mom's car."

"Who does?"

"Dad."

"Where does he keep them?"

"On his dresser."

"Maybe she would dare to sneak in there and get them."

"You've got to be kidding."

"I'm not, and I hope she dares, because I don't."

"Me either." Daniel admitted. "I think I'd rather just tell

38

Mom and Dad in the morning and take our chances."

"Sure! You haven't done anything wrong. I'm the one who's going to get into all the trouble."

"Well, I'm not asking Maryann," Daniel said.

"Then I will."

Yolanda marched silently into the kitchen and up the stairs, her flashlight in her hand. Daniel was not far behind. "Yo-Yo, be quiet," he kept whispering. She didn't even turn around.

"I have nothing to lose," she said loudly enough so he could hear her even though he was behind her. She stopped front of Maryann's door and knocked softly three times. When she heard the bed covers rustling, she opened the door and spoke quickly, "Maryann, it's me—Yo-Yo."

"You scared me, Yo-Yo," Maryann said.

Yolanda went in and sat on the bed. "I'm sorry," she said, "but I need your help." She told Maryann the whole story, from the shack in the woods to the slamming of the trunk. Only when Maryann's eyes became adjusted to the light did she notice Daniel standing in the doorway.

When she was fully awake and sitting up, she reached out and put a hand on each of Yolanda's shoulders. "I'll do what I can to get that box out of the trunk," she said. "But I won't take Dad's keys from his room."

"Then how will you get into the trunk?"

"Never mind. Just listen. I think I can get the box out for you, but before you try to open it again, you have to listen to what I have to say."

"Which is what?"

"I'll tell you in the garage, after we get the box out. Fair enough?"

"I guess."

"You want my help or not?"

"Of course I do, Maryann. Please don't get angry with me."

"I'm not angry with you, Yo-Yo. I just want you to learn something from this."

"I think I have already. Don't walk in the woods alone."

"Wait in the hall for me," Maryann said. "And whatever you do, don't wake up anyone else."

When Maryann came out, she was wearing sneakers and jeans and a sweater. Her hair was in a bun. But to Yolanda she still looked beautiful as always.

Her older sister led them quietly down the stairs. They tiptoed through the kitchen and into the garage. She went straight to her mother's car and crawled into the back seat, apparently not concerned that the inside light came on.

She put both hands on the back of the seat and gave a sharp tug. "I saw Dad do this once," she said. The seat back loosened and fell forward. "Let me have the flashlight."

Daniel handed it in, his eyes wide. He couldn't believe Maryann knew how to do this! "I can reach the box from here," she said, handing the keys out behind her without looking. As Daniel took them, she grunted. "Oh! It is heavy! Good grief, Yo-Yo, how did you ever get it home?"

She gave up trying to slide it out through the back seat. After replacing everything, she took the keys and opened the trunk. She and Daniel lifted it out and set it on the floor. The two younger children looked up at her, expecting her to magically open it as well.

"Ready for your part of the deal?" Maryann asked.

They both nodded.

"You mean just listening?" Yolanda said.

"That's right," she said. "Sit down." They dropped to the floor. Maryann settled down with her back to the back bumper of her mother's car, her feet flat on the floor and her knees raised. She wrapped her arms around her knees and clasped her hands, appearing deep in thought.

"You stole that box, Yolanda," she said suddenly.

"What?"

"Just listen. You broke into that house—"

"It was a shack!"

"You agreed to listen! You broke into that place and—"

"The window was unlocked!"

40

"But you were not invited. Do you think if someone came in our house through an unlocked window they wouldn't be in trouble?"

Yolanda didn't answer.

"You broke into that place and stole the box. And you damaged property that didn't belong to you."

"But no one owns that shack!"

"You don't know that. Someone uses it. And even if it doesn't belong to them, it certainly doesn't belong to you. You know that box belongs to others, even if they don't own the shack where they keep it. Don't you?"

Again, Yolanda didn't answer.

"Don't you, Yo-Yo?" Maryann pressed.

Yolanda nodded.

"So what are you going to do, Yolanda?"

Yolanda hated when Maryann called her that. No one could say "Yo-Yo" better than Maryann. But when she said "Yolanda" she sounded like a mother. Especially when she was bawling her out.

"What do you mean, what am I going to do? I was hoping to find out what's inside the box."

"You haven't heard what I've been saying, have you?"

"I have."

"Then how can you think you have the right to open a box that doesn't belong to you?"

"But it's got stolen money in it, Maryann," Daniel said.

"You don't know that! And even if you did, what makes you two the police? Who gave you the right to take the evidence and investigate the case?"

They both sat silent.

"So what are you going to do?" she asked. No one spoke for almost a minute. Maryann stared first at one and then the other. "Well?" she said.

Yolanda stood and paced. "You mean you aren't just dying to know what's in that box?" she asked. "Don't you want to know how much money those bullies have taken from the elementary school kids?"

Maryann shook her head. "I'm curious, yes. It would make me happy to find out that it's *not* stolen money. But, you see, I don't have the right to break into the box," she said.

Yolanda sat down next to Daniel and spoke to him. "I just want to know what's in the box," she said.

"Me too," he said looking sheepishly at Maryann.

She scowled at them, pressing her lips together and slowly shaking her head.

7

Sneaking Back

Maryann stood and backed herself up onto the trunk of the car, her feet resting on the bumper. She looked sad. "Daniel," she began slowly, "you know better."

"Me?" he said, hurt. "Why me? I didn't steal the box!"

"I didn't steal it either!" Yolanda shouted, bursting into tears.

"You did, too!" Daniel said. "Maryann is right! It didn't belong to you."

"Both of you be quiet," Maryann whispered. "Daniel, stop it! You're as guilty as she is. You tried everything you knew to get into the box. You knew good and well it was the wrong thing to do.

"You need to be an example to Yolanda. You grew up in this family, and you've been in trouble more than once, just like I have. But by now you know the difference between right and wrong, even if Yolanda doesn't.

"You're a Christian, Daniel. Do you think God is happy about you trying to break into someone else's property?"

Maryann stopped lecturing. Daniel was glad. He knew she was right, but he hated it when she preached at him. He

43

loved her, and he wanted her help. Nothing was worse than when she made him feel guilty.

"Am I right, Daniel?"

He looked at the floor, then nodded.

"So what are you going to do?" she asked again.

"I'm going to be a good example to Yo-Yo and tell her to do the right thing."

"Which is?"

"To tell Mom and Dad and take her punishment."

"Ha!" Maryann said. "And you get off with nothing?"

"What do you think we should do then, Miss Know-It-All?" Daniel asked. He was sorry he said it as soon as it came out of his mouth.

"I don't need to take that from you, Daniel. You want me to put the box back in the trunk and toss the keys in with it, and let you two work it out with Mom and Dad? I came down here and helped you because you asked me to. Your part of the bargain was to listen."

"Yeah, and listen to how wrong we've been. And how we've messed everything up."

"Well, haven't you?"

"Yes!" Yolanda said. "Stop talking to him and tell me what to do. I agree I was wrong. I didn't even think about it. But now I feel terrible—and I don't care about the box. I don't care if I ever find out what's in it. I don't even want to see it again."

"You have to see it to take it back," Maryann said.

"Take it back?" Yolanda said. "No way. No. No."

"Then Mom and Dad have to know. Otherwise, you can make things right yourself. I'll lend you some money to leave in the shack with the box for the damage you did to the window and the box. And you two can pay me back whenever you can."

"I have to pay you back?" Daniel yelped. "What'd I do?"

"You had as much to do with wrecking the box as Yolanda did," Maryann said. "Now that's the deal. Ten dollars should cover it. Write a note. Apologize for taking the box and damaging it and the window. I'll give you ten dollars to put in with the note."

"And then we're supposed to lug this thing back into the woods?" Yolanda asked. "And put it back under the kitchen sink?"

"Not necessarily under the sink. You'd better put it where they'll find it."

"But you're really telling us to take it back?"

"Of course."

"When?"

"As soon as possible. Before morning, certainly."

"Will you drive us?"

"How can I do that without waking up the whole house?"

"Will you walk with us?"

Maryann looked toward the ceiling and rubbed her eyes. Daniel and Yolanda knew they had her then.

"Please, please," they begged.

"Why not?" she said. "I'll never get back to sleep now anyway."

They jumped around, thanking her. She had to remind them to be quiet.

"But you both have to tell me, and mean it, that you really see you were wrong."

Daniel and Yolanda looked at each other, but didn't say anything. Finally, they nodded, but they didn't convince Maryann. "You two are going to get in real trouble someday if you don't learn from this. Now get dressed and keep quiet."

When they were ready to leave, Maryann tied a long piece of clothesline rope around the backpack. She carried it herself for the first several blocks. Then she let Yolanda and Daniel carry it together, until they got near the woods.

"You lead the way, Yo-Yo," she said. They slipped into the trees from the path near the road. It was the middle of the night, and they hadn't seen one car.

They had brought only one flashlight. The decided not

to use it until they were deeper into the woods. That way it would not be seen from the road. They stumbled about, trying to find the area near the creek. They could hear the water. But they couldn't see well enough to be sure they weren't about to fall in.

Finally, Maryann told Daniel to turn on the light. Within a few minutes, Yolanda had led them through the dense underbrush to the clearing where the shack was partially hidden.

"Cut the light, Daniel," Maryann said. "Quick!"

"Why?"

"Just do it!" she whispered frantically.

He turned it out. "What's the matter?" he asked.

"I saw something."

"What'd you see?"

"Another light."

"Where."

"Over there."

"It's too dark to see where you're pointing. Where?"

"To your right about fifty feet."

"I didn't see anything." Daniel said.

"Me either," Yolanda said.

"Maybe I didn't either," Maryann admitted. "But keep that light off for a while, just in case. There! There it was again! There *is* someone over there, Daniel! Didn't you see it that time?"

"No."

"Keep watching."

"I saw it," Yolanda said, a little too loudly.

"Shh!"

"Well, I did!" she said. "Right where you said. And there it is again!"

"I saw it!" Daniel said. "Who do you think it is, Maryann?"

"I have no idea. Let's find out."

"Are you sure you want to?"

"No, but let's move that way anyway. And let's stay together."

"Of course!" Yolanda said, as if there was no other choice. "What should we do with the box?"

"Leave it right here. We can find our way back here."

They crept through the bushes toward where the light had been. They saw it several more times before they got close enough to make out where it was coming from. Two teenage boys in warm jackets sat on wooden chairs outside the shack. They warmed themselves by rubbing their arms and shaking their legs from time to time. And every once in a while, one of them would flash his light into the sky or up a tree or somewhere.

"What's he looking for?" Yolanda whispered.

"I don't think he's looking for anything," Maryann said. "I think he's just bored. It looks as if they're on guard duty or something. They have nothing better to do than chat and shine their lights every once in a while. I'm going to get closer to try to hear them. Be ready to run if they hear us. We can find our way out, can't we? You do remember the way?"

Daniel and Yolanda nodded. But it was clear they weren't thrilled about Maryann getting any closer to the boys. What if they were some of the bullies who had stolen the money in the first place—and were just waiting for the robbers to return to the scene of the crime? What might they do to her?

Maryann moved around to the back of the shack, and all the way up the other side. Now Daniel and Yolanda couldn't call to her, or signal her, or anything, without being noticed by the boys on guard. They were on the creek side of the guards, and Maryann was on the other side.

Suddenly, Daniel grew bold. "I want to hear what they're saying, too," he said.

"What?" Yolanda asked. "And leave me here? Forget it. If you leave, I'll yell."

"And get Maryann killed? You wouldn't."

"Just don't leave me," she said.

"All right," he said, "then you're coming with me."

"Up to where Maryann is? She said to wait here and be ready to run. Anyway if we all get on that side of the shack, it's a lot longer way out of the woods. They'd catch us for sure."

"Then let's just move up closer, Yo-Yo," he said. "I want to hear what they're talking about." He took her hand and pulled her closer to the clearing.

8

Maryann Disappears

Daniel and Yolanda slowed and dropped to their stomachs, crawling the last ten feet or so. Finally they were at the edge of the bushes near the clearing, not far from the older boys.

The boys were rocking and humming and picking up stones and tossing them at trees. The taller one said, "You really think anyone'll show up tonight?"

"Here, you mean?" the other asked. "Nah. Probably not. But we have to stay here until Bo comes back. We're never gonna see that money again, you know."

"I know."

"Those junior highers probably got it."

"Probably. Wonder how long they've known about this place."

The other shrugged. Then he sat up straight and stared into the bushes. Yolanda had shifted her weight and cracked some twigs. If she and Daniel had stayed still, the teenagers would have lost interest in the noise. But Daniel said, "Shh," a little too loudly. Then he started backing away making some noise of his own.

The first boy started to say something, but the other held up his hand for silence. Still staring into the bushes, he stood and began to edge toward them. From across the way, Maryann could tell that her younger brother and sister had been heard.

To distract the teenagers, she tossed a small rock behind one of them and then the other. Now both were on their feet, scuffing and darting back and forth with flashlights on.

But Maryann's plan had not worked. The one still couldn't take his eyes off the bushes. He had heard something there for sure. No matter where those annoying rocks were coming from, he was going to check it out.

He jogged toward Daniel and Yolanda, making them crawl backward. Then they stood, turned, and scurried through the woods.

"Over here!" the teen yelled to his companion.

But Maryann's high-pitched scream pierced the blackness. "Run, kids! Run! Don't you stop!" She had screamed it so loud that it stopped the boys in their tracks. They whirled around to see where the scream had come from. Daniel too looked over his shoulder as he followed Yolanda toward the creek bed. He saw lights waving about. He thought he saw Maryann running the other way through the woods.

"She'll never get out that way, Daniel!" Yolanda cried. "How will she find the main path in the dark? They'll catch her!"

Daniel shined his flashlight along a row of trees high on the bank of the creek so they could keep moving. "We can't help her," he said.

"Why not?"

"What would we do against those guys?"

"There'd be three of us," she said. But she made no turn to run after Maryann.

"But they're waiting for someone named Bo," Daniel said. "Then there'd be three of them—and then what would we do?"

Yolanda didn't answer. Her breathing was so fast she couldn't speak anymore. They just ran and ran. She remembered having run the same way the afternoon before. When Daniel slowed to figure out where to go, she just charged on by and led him out to the path near the bus stop.

They stopped and huffed and puffed. Putting their hands on their hips, they bent over at the waist to help them breathe better. "If any cars come, we have to move back in behind the trees," Daniel said.

"You know what this reminds me of?" she said. "When we ran off to Grandpa's without anybody knowing."

"Don't remind me. This time we're doing what Maryann said we should—so we can't get into trouble."

"Oh yeah? What if something happens to her? Now I really know I was wrong taking that box."

"The box!" he said. "Where is it? We have to go back. We have to find it!"

"Daniel, we can't go back! We have to go home and get help for Maryann. We can take care of the box later."

A car came around the curve. Daniel pulled Yolanda into the woods. "Those guys didn't seem like bad guys, did they, Yo-Yo? We have to hope they won't hurt Maryann, even if they do catch her—which they probably won't. Cheerleaders are in good shape, you know. She's an awfully fast runner."

Yolanda was almost jumping. She wanted to do something other than just stand around. "So what are we going to do, Daniel? Tell me, and I'll help!"

"We're going to find that box and put it back in the shack before anyone comes back."

"Why are you more worried about the box than about Maryann?" Yolanda asked.

"Because if anything does happen to Maryann, we'd better be sure we did what she told us to do."

"That's all you're worried about, Daniel? Not getting into trouble?"

51

"I'm worried about Maryann, too!" he shouted. "But there's nothing we can do about her now. We can find that box, though, so let's go."

"I don't want to! I want to go home."

"Then go! I'm looking for the box before someone else finds it."

Daniel headed into the woods. Yolanda looked toward the road, then back at him. She quickly followed him so he wouldn't get too far ahead. "I'm right behind you," she said. "But I think we're going to be in trouble."

He didn't answer, but she knew he was glad to have her along. She prayed that Maryann would find her way out and make it home.

The best thing of all that could happen would be for Maryann to escape from the woods and be OK. They could find the box, return it to the shack, and make it home soon enough after Maryann so she wouldn't worry.

Yolanda was afraid that was hoping for a little too much. But she wasn't afraid to pray for it. That's what everybody else in her new family seemed to do all the time.

It was darker and colder than ever in the woods now. And they were tired from their running. They walked slower and slower. They disagreed about where they had been when they dropped the box. They split up for a while. Looking in different places, they whistled to keep track of each other.

Every once in a while they'd stop to listen for anything strange. But they heard nothing. No one. Not a sound except for what you'd expect to hear in the woods in the middle of the night.

A half hour later, Daniel was no longer excited about finding and returning the box. "We might as well go," he said.

Yolanda nodded, but she didn't say anything. Disappointedly, they trudged back toward the road. When they were almost to the hedge that separated the woods from the road, they heard fast footsteps crashing toward them.

They froze, not knowing which way to turn. They started toward the road. Then they heard what sounded like whimpering. Whoever was bounding toward them was crying. They ran different directions, then back to each other, then together toward the road again. By then the racing steps were upon them, and they could hear Maryann crying, "Please be all right, Daniel and Yo-Yo. Please be all right!"

"We're all right!" they yelled together.

"We're here!" Yolanda called.

"And we're all right," Daniel added.

Maryann fell to her knees, exhausted and weeping. She held out her hands without looking up. And they both came near so she could hug them. "I was so worried about you," she said.

"We were worried about you, too." Yolanda said. "At least I was. How did you get away?"

When Maryann could catch her breath, she laughed and said, "I ran those guys around for at least a mile. I got way ahead of them and stopped. And when they came near I threw rocks behind them. They ran after the noises. And then I ran around behind them and chased them, barking like a dog."

"Why couldn't we hear you?" Daniel asked.

"I don't know—I was loud enough. But we were way over past the main path on the other side. I think I scared those guys out of the woods."

"We couldn't find the box," Yolanda said.

"We'll find it," Maryann said. "We're not going home till we put that box back. You've got to make this thing right."

"Well, where were we standing when you first noticed the flashlight?" Daniel said. "I'm afraid someone's already taken the box."

"They couldn't have," she said. "You two were over here. And I was on the other side. No one's been in between. C'mon, I'll show you where."

They kicked around in the tall grass beyond the creek. It was Daniel who found the box again. "Here!" he called.

The clothesline was still in place. By being careful, the

three of them were able to share the load. Even Maryann was too tired to carry it herself.

They moved along at a steady pace, stopping occasionally to listen for noises. "Those guys won't be back tonight," she said. "They may never come back."

Daniel and Yolanda smiled. They were proud of their big sister.

As they reached the shack, Yolanda pointed out the window she had found unlocked—the one she had broken. But when they dragged the box up next to it, Maryann found solid glass.

"It's not broken, Yo-Yo. Are you sure this was the window?"

"Of course! Isn't that the kitchen?"

Maryann shined Daniel's light in the window. She pressed her nose up against it for a closer look. "Yup. That's the kitchen." She tried the window.

"Not only is it not broken, Yo-Yo—it's locked, too."

9

The Surprise

"Leave the box outside the door with the note?"
"No," she said. "We can't take the risk. The owners might come back to a note and no box."

"But who else knows about the shack?" Yolanda asked.

"Who knows? Did those boys on guard here tonight look like the kids who stole your dollar?"

Yolanda shook her head.

Maryann stood thinking a moment. "We'll take the box back home and leave the note."

"And the ten dollars?" Daniel said.

"No. Too risky."

"But the note says Yo-Yo's sorry about taking the box. It doesn't tell them where to come and get it."

Maryann looked upset. "And we don't have anything to write with, do we?"

"Nope," Daniel said, fishing in his empty pockets.

"Nope," Yolanda said. "Oh, yes! Yes, we do!"

"We do?"

"In my backpack! I have two pens and a pencil. Take your pick."

Maryann rifled through the backpack and pulled out a

stubby pencil. She crossed out the note Yolanda had written, She wrote on the back of the sheet: "Pick up your damaged, but unopened, box and payment for your broken window at 3537 Gables Road after 7 tonight. Ask for Maryann."

"Who lives there?" Daniel asked.

"Suzy, my friend. She's a cheerleader, too. I'll go there after practice."

"But we have to be there," Yolanda said. "I have to at least. This was all my fault. I want to find out who owns the box—and find out if I can get my money back."

"Then I'll ask Mom if you two can go with me on an errand if I have you back about eight. I'm sure she'll let you."

The three Bradfords made it home much faster than they made it to the woods, though they were still lugging the heavy box.

For some reason it seemed more difficult to sneak back into the house than it had to sneak out. But they made it. No one stirred. They were safe, and sound asleep, when Mr. Bradford got up at six o'clock for his three-mile run.

That afternoon, after school, Yolanda went directly to the bus. But she kept her eyes open. She searched for any face that looked like the junior high boy and girl who stole her money or like the boys—they could have been older—who were guarding the shack.

She saw some juniors highers who were dressed like the boy and girl. They were following smaller kids and making fun of them. She hoped the younger ones would be careful and stay in the open or get on a bus.

She couldn't really help them, or even warn them. She had promised herself, her mother, and her sister that she would come straight home on the bus.

Daniel arrived home at just after six o'clock, excited about having made the sixth-grade basketball team.

Jim was going to be late. He was at varsity practice.

"I have to run over to Suzy's for a little while after dinner, Mom," Maryann said. "Can Daniel and Yo-Yo come along, if I promise to have them back by eight?"

56

"I suppose, if they want to," she said.

"I do," they said together, a little too quickly.

"Why?" Mrs. Bradford said. "What's going on over there?"

"They have video games."

"Oh, I don't want Daniel and Yo-Yo getting interested in that stuff, Maryann."

"Oh, Mom. We won't be there long. Is it all right?"

"I guess—if schoolwork is done first and you're all home by eight."

Daniel and Yolanda ran to do their schoolwork.

Suzy, Maryann's friend, was tiny with black hair almost to her waist.

"You're Daniel, huh?" she said. "You a ballplayer like your big brother?"

Daniel nodded, but he didn't say anything.

To Yolanda, Suzy said, "You are gorgeous—just like Maryann said! Just wait till you're in high school!"

Yolanda wasn't quite sure what Suzy meant by that. But she was too nervous about the box to worry about it anyway. As they sat awkwardly in the living room, Suzy said, "So I suppose you heard about the fire!"

The Bradfords looked at each other.

"No," Maryann said. "What fire? Where?"

"After school—during practice. I heard there was a fire in the woods, not too far from your house."

"You're kidding! I heard fire engines during practice. But they must have cleared out by the time I got home. Who told you this?"

"Your brother."

"Jim?"

"Yes."

"He called you but didn't call his own family?"

"Well, he's not taking his own family out this weekend, is he?"

"Oh. No. I didn't know. So, anyway, what was the fire all about? A brush fire?"

"No, some building by the creek. Nobody was hurt. In fact, no one was there, I guess. Jim says nobody lived there. He says the sophomore football team has used it as a sort of meeting place for a while, because they've got a project going."

Maryann was almost speechless. "A project?"

"Yeah. Jim says their coach's wife is sick and the team has been doing odd jobs in their spare time to get money to give him for her medical bills. The team captain, Bo Head, is in charge of it all. But apparently the money was stolen yesterday. The team thinks whoever stole it came back and burned the building down, too. The guys had just had a window or something repaired. They were even guarding the place for most of the night, but it happened anyway—this afternoon."

By now Yolanda was almost in tears. Daniel sat wide-eyed, and Maryann was bursting with their story. She told Suzy everything.

"So, Bo will probably be coming here at eight," Suzy said. "Well, that'll be nice. I wonder if he'll open the box and let us know how much was in it."

"But, Suzy," Maryann said, "it won't be the football team coming for the box tonight. It'll be whoever found the note—and probably whoever burned down the shack."

Yolanda was confused. She couldn't make it all make sense. "You mean when I was taking the box from the shack, the kids I heard were the football team—and not the bullies?"

"We don't know," Maryann said. "But if they got into the shack with a key, it was probably the football team."

"But I heard girls' voices, too."

"Probably some girl friends," Suzy said. "I don't think the cheerleaders were in on this."

"No, we weren't," Maryann said. "I wish we had been. I didn't even know about the coach's wife."

"Hardly anyone does," Suzy said. "The coach doesn't even know that the players know."

Daniel had a puzzled look on his face. "Maryann, where

did those two come from who stole Yolanda's money yesterday?"

Suzy and Maryann looked at each other. "We're just guessing," Maryann said, "but maybe they hadn't discovered the shack yet. Maybe they just ran through the woods. Or heard the noise at the shack. Or just heard Yo-Yo moving toward the road. Maybe they weren't in the woods at all."

"Yes, they were!" Yolanda said. "I heard them coming up on me. And then when I got onto the path, they came up behind me."

"But did you see them come from the woods? They didn't see *you* come from the woods. They believed you when you said you had just been walking the path beside the woods."

"That's true," Yolanda said. "They did. But you don't think they were in the woods? Who was chasing me through the woods then?"

"Maybe some of the football players."

"Right," Suzy said. "And maybe the bullies who took your money went back into the woods. Maybe they discovered the shack with its broken window and were sneaking around in there."

"And, maybe the football players ran them off. Then they discovered their box was missing—and figured it was those kids who had stolen it," Maryann guessed.

"But wouldn't the football team have been practicing yesterday?" Daniel asked.

"No. They had a game the day before, so they just had a meeting after school."

Daniel still wasn't sure they were right. "Then the box of money we thought belonged to the bullies really belongs to the sophomore football team? And now they think someone stole it and burned down their shack?"

Maryann and Suzy nodded.

"We're only guessing," Suzy said. "But it makes sense."

"Well," Yolanda said, her voice weak and shaky, "whoever burned down the shack probably found our note. He'll come over here tonight for the box."

Suzy, looking a little worried, said, "I love a mystery. I'm just not sure I want some thieves having my address—especially with my parents out of town."

"I never thought of that, Suzy," Maryann said. "I never should have used your address without asking."

"That's all right," Suzy said.

Daniel looked out the window into the blackness of the early fall evening. He didn't even know what he was looking for.

"Shouldn't we call for some help?" he asked.

"I think we can handle it," Maryann said.

"Me, too," Suzy said. But she didn't sound quite sure.

"Shouldn't you at least turn on the front light?" Daniel suggested.

"I don't know," Suzy said. "Maybe if the light is off they won't come to the door."

Everyone chuckled, but Suzy jumped up and put it on anyway.

Just as she was returning to the living room and asking if anyone wanted anything to drink, the doorbell rang.

10

Visit from Robbers

"What do we do?" Maryann asked. She was suddenly looking to Suzy for help since it was her home—never minding the fact that this was Maryann's own idea. "I mean, uh, I was thinking that we were going to apologize for what Yo-Yo and Daniel had done. But what if it's the ones who burned down the shack and wanted to steal the money for themselves?"

Suzy ran to the door and called out, "Just a minute!"

"No rush!" came the reply. "It's just me!"

"Just who?"

"Thanks a lot! Just Jim!"

Suzy opened the door. "Oh, Jim! Come in! What are you doing here? You know I'm not supposed to have any guys over when my parents aren't home."

"I know. But I figured if my brother and sisters were here, it would be all right."

"Sure it is! Sit down."

"Boy, are we glad you're here," Yolanda said. "Maryann lost her courage at the last minute."

"Well, Mom said you were over here. And I didn't want

to pass up the chance for a quick visit." He winked at Suzy, who smiled. "Maryann lost her courage about what?"

Maryann let Yolanda tell the story. Without a word, Jim stood. "Maybe we can follow these guys. That is, unless the football players found the note. Then we'll just give 'em the box."

"You mean you'd let the bullies take the box? Even though you know it isn't theirs?" Daniel asked.

"We won't let'em out of our sight," Jim said. "I owe them one for hassling Yo-Yo anyway."

"You gonna smash 'em for me, Jim?" Yolanda asked.

"Nah. We'll just think of a way to take care of this stealing and vandalism without hurting anyone—and without making the bad kids even worse off."

"What do you mean?"

"I mean we have to do something nice for them. Of course, if we catch them doing something wrong, they're going to pay for it. But like Maryann told you two last night, you did wrong and you have to make it right. Now what's the right thing to do, besides paying for the damage and returning the box?"

"Punching their lights out so they don't do it again," Daniel suggested.

Jim laughed. "I know how you feel, Dan. But is that what Maryann did when she found out what *you* had done?"

"No. She made us do the right thing."

"What if she had yelled at you?"

"We would have been mad," Yolanda said.

"Sure you would have," Jim said.

"And I might not be so sorry that I smashed up the box trying to help Yo-Yo."

"Right. Would Maryann have helped you learn your lesson?"

"Not like we're learning it now," Daniel said. "I feel terrible about scaring those football players last night. They were just trying to guard their place and do something nice for their coach's wife."

"I feel even worse," Yolanda said. "Think of what I did. Stealing that money and breaking that window—and not even thinking I had done anything wrong. I even feel like the shack burning was my fault—if those kids did it just to cover their tracks and get the box. I wonder if they even know what's in the box."

"I'll bet they do," Jim said. "My guess is that they had been watching the football players and their place. They were just waiting for the chance to get in there."

"Then maybe they were the ones who chased me out of the woods?" Yolanda asked.

"Maybe. But it might have been the football players. It might have been both. Maybe they were coming to the shack while the bullies were nosing around, and they both wound up running through the woods. But Maryann did the right thing. She didn't yell. She helped you see how you were wrong."

"And that's what you think we should do with the bullies, if they show up?" Maryann said.

"Yes, but I'm not sure quite how to do it," he said. "The best thing would be for them to see that they've been wrong, pay for it, and still know that somebody cares about them."

"I don't care about them," Yolanda said. "I hate them."

Maryann flinched, but Jim said, "I know how you feel. That's how I would feel, too, if I hadn't been taught better."

"You mean I don't know better?" Yolanda asked. "I think you might feel the same way if you'd been kicked and had a dollar stolen."

"I know," Jim said. "I'm not blaming you for how you feel, Yo-Yo. But the fact is that it isn't right. It isn't the way Jesus would feel about them."

"He would let them get away with everything they've done—stealing from little kids, probably burning down someone's hideout, and saying the box is theirs—which is what you know they'll do?"

"No, God never lets people get away with things. But He does let them know that He loves them and cares about them. And that He wants them to change and live for Him."

"Sounds like you want to let them off," Yolanda said.

"No, it doesn't," Daniel said. "I think Jim's right."

"We all know he's right," Maryann said. "We have to do something that will not just show them that they're wrong, which they probably already know. We have to do something that will also surprise them."

"Surprise them?" Yolanda said. "I'd like to surprise one of them right in the mouth."

"I know," Jim said. "That's the way we feel when we just think of ourselves. But if you were thinking about what God would do, how He would treat them, would you still want to hurt them?"

Yolanda shrugged.

"I know you're not trying to be mean," Jim said. "But you probably haven't seen how people react when they're loved along with being punished for what they've done."

"I hadn't thought about it," Maryann said, "but that is what I was doing last night with you and Daniel. I could have just gotten mad and told you off. It was frustrating to have to talk you into seeing that you were wrong and needed to make things right. But you reacted better than you would have the other way. You admitted that yourselves."

Yolanda didn't know what to think or say.

"Yolanda, you do know how people feel when they're loved rather than just punished." Suzy said. "I know it's none of my business, but don't you feel a lot better now that you're in a family of people who love you, rather than in a big orphanage where they just take care of you."

Yolanda nodded. "You think those bullies feel like orphans and need someone to love them?" she asked. "I don't remember any orphans being that bad."

"I do," Daniel said. "Remember that kid who tore up my ten-speed?"

It was as if a light came on in Yolanda's mind. "That's right," she said. "And you're right, too, Suzy. Only I'm not sure I won't want to smash one of those kids if I see them again. Of course, if you're all going to be nice to them I might not get the chance."

Everyone smiled, hoping Yolanda would learn something if the bad kids showed up. But they were all a little worried, too. Then Jim explained his plan.

If anyone except the sophomore football team came to the door asking for Maryann, she would give them the box. She would apologize for what happened, just as if it belonged to them. Then Jim and Suzy and Maryann and Daniel and Yolanda would follow them and see if they could talk to their whole gang, wherever they had their meeting place.

"Someone's coming up the walk," Daniel announced.

"Who it it?" Jim asked. Suzy turned the living room lights off and everyone crowded around the window.

"They look like some of the kids who steal lunch money," Daniel said. "Do you recognize them, Yo-Yo?"

She squinted and stared as the young boy and girl walked slowly up the walk. "I sure do," she said. "Those are the two who stole my dollar and kicked me yesterday."

11

"Let's Have the Box!"

Yolanda wanted Jim to run to the door and smash the two junior highers for having stolen her money and kicked her. But Jim signaled that Suzy should go to the door and act natural.

The boy asked for Maryann.

"And who may I say is calling?" Suzy asked.

"What?"

"Who are you?"

"What do you mean, who are we? What's it to you, if you're not Maryann?"

"I'm the one who's going to get Maryann for you, if you tell me who you are."

The boy looked disgusted. "We're the ones who found her note," he said. "She'll know what it's all about."

"Her note?"

"Yes! Is she here?"

"Yes, and I'll get her, as soon as you tell me your names."

"I'm C.C., and this is Mattie," he said. "Now get her, will ya?"

"Won't you come in, C.C. and Mattie?"

"Nah, we don't wanna come in. Just tell her to fork over the box."

Maryann came to the door. "I didn't take your box," she said. "My little sister did. And she wants to tell you how sorry she is. My little brother damaged the box, too, and he's sorry about that. But before I get them so they can apologize, maybe you could describe the box to me. That way I can be sure you're the owners."

"What are you talking about? Either your brother and sister took our box or they didn't. Now let's have it!"

"Just tell me what it looks like."

"It's a box. A box! What can a box look like? It's a plain, old box!"

"No, it isn't. Tell me more."

"It's wood," he said.

"It's cardboard," Mattie said.

"You're both wrong," Suzy said. "I don't think the box is yours."

"The box is ours," C.C. said. "And if we don't come back with it, we're going to be in big trouble. I know what the box looks like. It's about this big. It's made of dark green metal. It has a padlock, and it weighs over thirty pounds."

Maryann was startled. He was right! "Just a minute," she said. "Wait right here."

She ran back in to tell Jim. "Maybe they really do own the box," she whispered. "But why did he try to make me think they didn't?"

"They don't," Jim said quickly. "That box and the money belong to the sophomore football team. Maybe these two, and the gang they come from, have seen the box before. Maybe they were about to take it just before Yo-Yo stole it. Go ahead and give it to them. We'll follow them to see who they run with. Better be ready to roll when they leave."

The door bell rang again, and C.C. hollered, "Hey! What's going on? Let's have the box!"

Maryann pulled Daniel and Yolanda to the door, then lugged the box out.

67

"These are my brother and sister," she said. "And they want to apologize for—"

"Forget the apologies. We forgive you," C.C. said, yanking the box from Maryann and almost falling under its weight. He quickly swung it onto his shoulder and held his other hand straight out for balance.

As he started to walk away, Yolanda said, "You don't remember me, do you?"

He turned around slowly, squinting at her. "Should I?" he asked, as Mattie also gave her a good looking over.

"We got a buck off her last night," she said.

He nodded slowly. "So we borrowed a dollar. What about it?"

"You borrowed it?" Yolanda said.

"Yeah, what about it?"

"You also kicked me."

"Well, you weren't real quick to hand over the buck, all right?"

"No, it's not all right. I want my dollar back"

C.C. and Mattie smiled sneeringly at her. C.C. let the box slide from his shoulder into his hands. He placed it slowly on the sidewalk. He turned and stuck out his hand to Mattie. She pulled a key from her tiny handbag and gave it to him.

He unlocked the padlock and opened the box. In the dim light from the porch light, Yolanda and Daniel and Maryann saw what looked like hundreds of dollars—plus a lot of change.

"Here's a dollar for your dollar," C.C. said, removing two from the box. "And one for your shin. All right?"

"I don't take stolen money," Yolanda said, "I know where you got that—"

"Just a minute, Yo-Yo," Maryann said. "Take your dollar, and we'll talk about this later."

Yolanda took one dollar, C.C. closed and locked the box with a great flourish, hoisted it onto his shoulder again, and he and Mattie went off down the street.

Maryann, Daniel, and Yolanda dashed back into the house, just as Jim and Suzy headed out the back door to the car. Maryann caught up to Jim and said, "The girl had the key to the box! Where would she have gotten that?"

"I have no idea," Jim said. "But we're going to find out."

Jim drove the station wagon slowly down the driveway. They followed C.C. and Mattie from a long distance. Two blocks away, they climbed into the back door of a Buick that was at least as old as they were.

"Now we're getting somewhere," Jim said. "I knew they had to have older friends. Got to keep our distance without losing them."

Daniel was enjoying the excitement, though he was a little scared. But Yolanda was troubled. She worried about her own thoughts. She worried about how differently she and Jim treated the same problem. She still didn't know whether she wanted to help these bad kids or just see them punished.

She'd had enough wrong treatment in her life. There were times when she wanted to explode—and not at just whatever seemed to be bothering her at that moment. Whether it was Daniel teasing her, or her losing something, or bullies stealing her dollar and kicking her, she wanted to tear into someone and take out all the hate and bitterness that had built up in her over the years spent in homes for children.

Where were her real parents? Where were her real brothers and sisters? What had she done that was so terrible that she deserved to live like that? Yes, there were times when she would just as soon take a baseball bat to the head of someone who gave her a bad time.

The idea of loving that kind of a person was something new to her. She knew what it was to love her little friends and leaders at the home—those who had been especially kind to her.

And, of course, she loved her new brothers and sister, and her new parents—probably most of all—because they took her from the children's home and brought her into a wonderful family. She would have to tell them all about this.

But there was still something deep inside her, something that bothered her, something that scared her. It was anger. She wasn't sure where it came from or what to do about it. Maybe someone like C.C. or Mattie deserved a little of it for what they had done to her. But once she started dishing it out, she wasn't sure she could stop. She might give them more than they deserved. They might have to pay for *all* the bad things life seemed to have brought her.

And Yolanda knew that wouldn't be right.

Jim carefully followed the old Buick, containing C.C., Mattie, and who knew who else, past the high school. They went farther into a dingy business district. And suddenly the Buick turned right into an alley.

"I'm going to stay back and let them go," Jim said. "The alleys around here don't go all the way through. Let's wait and see it they come out."

Ten minutes later, when the Buick had not reappeared, Jim had everyone head for the alley from different directions.

When they all arrived at the far end of the alley at about the same time, they found the Buick parked just outside a one-story concrete-block garage. A sign on the side door read: Cobra Car Club. Jim led the group around the side and to the back. There they saw light coming from two open windows near the roof of the old building

He quietly piled up barrels and cardboard boxes. Then he tried to climb up to peek in but the pile started to give way. Maryann tried. Even she was too heavy. Daniel tried. There just wasn't enough support.

Jim looked over his whole group. His eyes stopped on Yolanda. "Can you get up there?" he asked.

She nodded and started climbing.

The rickety pile stayed in place. As Yolanda reached the top and stood on her tiptoes, she could see clearly inside the garage. Not only that, she could hear everything, too.

12

Yo-Yo Faces the Gang

Yolanda counted ten people in the garage. It was lit by only one light fixture hanging from the middle of the ceiling. Mattie was one of three girls.

C.C. seemed to be the youngest boy. But there were at least two others that Yolanda guessed were in junior high. All ten were laughing as C.C. and Mattie described their adventure at Suzy's house.

"You shoulda seen the look on their faces when Mattie gave me the key and I popped that box open in nothing flat," C.C. said.

One of the older boys, a tall, lanky guy with a black sweater and grease-stained hands, leaped to his feet. He swore at C.C.

"You let 'em know you had the key, you idiot? You were s'posed to make it look like you didn't even know anything about the box. We wanted 'em to think we knew nothing about it!"

"I needed to tell them just to get the box!" C.C. said.

But the bigger boy swung at him with the back of his hand. He hit C.C. on the side of the head and knocked him to the floor. No one else moved. C.C. stood up and returned to his perch on the hood of a car.

The lanky one, whom the others called Fitch, opened the box and began counting the money.

"Not a bad haul, though, kid," Fitch said to C.C. It was his way of apologizing, Yolanda guessed.

Fitch counted out more than two hundred and fifty dollars.

Then, before Jim and Maryann's disbelieving eyes, Yolanda climbed through the window and stepped down onto a shaky metal auto-parts rack.

"Don't, Yo-Yo! Don't!" Jim whispered. He jumped up on the same pile that had supported Yolanda. It collapsed, sending him rolling into the alley.

"Are you all right?" Suzy asked, rushing to him.

"Yeah, but get around to the front. We've got to get in there."

They ran to the front of the garage and tried the overhead door. But it was locked.

The Cobra Car Club members didn't hear them trying to open it. Their eyes and ears were all on the tiny Mexican girl who had come in through the window.

They circled beneath her like big, prowling game cats. "Well, what have we here?"

"She's probably not alone," Fitch said. "Keep an eye on the doors."

But Jim had already opened the side door enough so he could hear what was going on.

"So, whatcha gonna do up there, honey?" Fitch said. "You coming down? Or you want me to come up there after you?"

Yolanda was amazed at how calmly she replied. "Don't get too close, or I'll make sure this thing comes down right on top of you."

"You will, huh?" Fitch said, laughing. He was enjoying himself.

Yolanda put her hands behind her on the wall and

pushed forward slightly with her feet. The huge rack, which looked like a bookcase filled with heavy objects, rocked back and forth.

Fitch jumped back a few feet. The smile was still on his face—but terror was in his eyes. "You push that thing over, sweetie, and you're comin' down with it. You know that?"

"I don't care," Yolanda said. "It'd be worth it."

"So what's your story, little one? What brings you to the club on this chilly night?"

"The money in that box," she said.

"What do you want with our money? You got yours back."

"It's not your money," she said. "It belongs to the sophomore football team, and it's for the coach's—"

"I'm on the sophomore football team," Nate Dysan said. "We know what it's for."

"Yeah," Fitch said. "How do you think we got the key? How do you think we knew where to find the box in the first place?"

"You mean you know all about what the money is for and you still—

"The money belongs to us now," Nate Dysan said.

"Tell your leader what it's for then," Yolanda challenged.

Nate Dysan didn't say anything.

"Yeah, Nate, tell me what's it's for. Something special? I thought you said it was just party money that no one would miss. They're all rich kids, you said, and they'd never miss it anyway."

"That's right," Nate said. "That's exactly right."

Yolanda began to climb down the metal back. Somehow she sensed she had a friend, or at least someone who would protect her, in Fitch. The way he was asking Nate Dysan questions made her think he wouldn't let anyone hurt her until she had delivered her message. And she was right.

Fitch backed up and watched her come down—then stepped forward and helped her the last several feet. The rest of the crowd was speechless and didn't move. Once she was on the ground, even Fitch just backed up and looked at this tough, brave, little girl.

She pointed at Nate. "Are you serious?" she said, looking at Fitch. "Is this guy really on the sophomore football team?"

"Yeah," Fitch growled, still staring at her with admiration. "What about it?"

"Then he knows what that money is for. Stealing lunch money and bus fares from little kids is bad enough," she said, pointing to C.C. and Mattie, who glared back at her. "But this guy knows what the money in the box is really for."

With that she was silent and looked deep into Fitch's eyes. He walked slowly toward Nate, while still looking at Yolanda. Then he turned and grabbed Nate's jacket in both fists and pulled him close.

"You're going to tell me about the money, Dysan," he said.

"I told you!"

"Don't lie to me, Nate. This girl doesn't climb through the window into this place unless she knows somethin' you're not telling me. Now what is it?"

Nate didn't say anything. Fitch walked him over to the wall and slammed him up against it. The back of his head thudded on the concrete. "I'm not askin' you again, Dysan."

"The coach," Nate said. "His wife's in the hospital. The team has been collecting that money to give to her."

Fitch looked as if he wanted to spit in Nate's face. Instead, he let go of him and let him drop to the floor in a heap. "And what's this about you and Mattie stealing money?" Fitch said. "You know the club rules. We only take money from people who won't miss it. You running with that bunch that steals from little kids? Are you?"

C.C. nodded miserably. "You're out of the club—both of you," Fitch said, moving toward him. "I can't believe you'd do that!"

C.C. reached behind him and grabbed the nearest weapon. It turned out to be a box of spark plugs. Yolanda wondered if he really thought he could defend himself with them against a big guy like Fitch. And she didn't know what to think of Fitch.

He had admitted that they took money. But he had some crazy idea of honor about it, almost like Robin Hood. He would rob from the rich but never from the poor. She knew it was wrong either way. But there was something she liked about him anyway.

C.C. hurled the box of plugs at Fitch, hitting him in the forehead. Fitch grabbed his head, but he charged C.C., who ran toward the side door.

Jim and everyone with him burst in. They wrestled C.C. to the ground. But they let him up as Fitch and his buddies approached.

Fitch looked at the blood on his hand and wiped it on C.C.'s jacket. He looked at Jim and Suzy and Maryann and Daniel, and chuckled. "So, it's party time, huh?" he said. He slid around behind C.C. and held the younger boy's arms back.

"Who wants the first shot at this creep? How about you, little girl?"

By now the members of the Cobra Car Club, even the girls, all had weapons made from auto parts. They surrounded Fitch and C.C. and glared at Jim and his friends. Yolanda walked slowly over to stand in front of C.C.

He was a pitiful sight now. His eyes were full of tears. He shook. His hands were pinned behind him by the bigger, stronger, Fitch. Yo-Yo wanted to kick him. She wanted to punch him. She wanted to take the tire iron from the hands of an older girl and hit him with it.

Over C.C.'s shoulder, she could see Fitch. His forehead bleeding. His mouth was curled into a sneer. For some strange reason, she knew he admired her. And she felt she was like him. And that, she knew, was her problem.

From the corner of her eye, she could also see her brother Jim. He stared at her. He obviously wondered what she was going to do with this chance for revenge. She couldn't read the look in his eyes. But she thought she knew what he would do.

And that's what she wanted to do, if only she could. She found herself praying silently, something she had hardly ever done before she had become a Bradford. All she wanted to do was the right thing.

"Let him go," she said.

Fitch was so startled that he loosened his grip.

She spoke ever so quietly to C.C. "Bring me the box," she said very low in her soft voice.

He stared at her without moving at first. Then he walked slowly to the box, shut and locked it, lugged it over to the floor next to her.

"Nate, you want to take it back to the team?" she asked.

Nate was still sitting next to the wall, crying. He waved a silent no at her and struggled to his feet. He walked around the crowd. Then he ran out the door and down the alley.

"Then I'll take it back, Fitch," she said. "If you promise not to hurt C.C. or Mattie."

Fitch cocked his head and looked at her as if he wasn't sure he had heard her right.

"Is it a deal?" she asked.

He nodded with a tight-lipped smile. "It's a deal."

No one there would ever forget the tiny Mexican girl who took over the Cobra Car Club one November night. Little Yolanda Trevino Bradford had done what was right—just because it was right.

Moody Press, a ministry of the Moody Bible Institute,
is designed for education, evangelization, and edification.
If we may assist you in knowing more about Christ
and the Christian life, please write us without obligation:
Moody Press, c/o MLM, Chicago, Illinois 60610.